DASHER
CAN'T WAIT FOR
CHRISTMAS

For Paige, Calvin, and Jack

Special thanks to Levi Stinson Freeman and Dave Banks

 First edition 2023. Library of Congress Catalog Card Number 2022922915. ISBN 978-1-5362-3013-0. This book was typeset in Brioso. The illustrations were created digitally. Candlewick Press, 99 Dover Street, Somerville, Massachusetts 02144. www.candlewick.com. Printed in Heshan, Guangdong, China. 23 24 25 26 27 28 LEO 10 9 8 7 6 5 4 3 2 1

DASHER
CAN'T WAIT FOR
CHRISTMAS

MATT TAVARES

CANDLEWICK PRESS

DASHER LIVES WITH HER FAMILY at the North Pole. She spends her days playing happily with the other reindeer. And in the evenings, before bedtime, they all practice flying under the glow of the North Star.

"Remember," Mama often says, "if you ever get lost, just look for the North Star. You can always find your way back home."

"Mama," Dasher asked one night, "how many sleeps till Christmas Eve?"

"Twelve," said Mama. "Every night, we're one night closer."

"Twelve sleeps?" asked Dasher. "That's too many!"

Dasher loves Christmas Eve. She loves hearing people sing Christmas carols. She loves seeing decorated trees through windows as she flies past. But her favorite thing of all is seeing the Christmas lights from high above.

"Soon," said Mama.

"I can't wait," said Dasher.

With each passing evening, the waiting grew more unbearable. Late one night, when the wind was howling and whistling through the trees and when Christmas Eve was only one sleep away, Dasher lay awake, too excited to close her eyes.

What was that sound? she wondered.

There it is again!

It sounded like Christmas carols! She stood up. She looked back at her sleeping family. *I'll be back before they even know I'm gone,* she said to herself. She started running. And then . . .

she took to the sky.

Dasher flew toward the music. But as the wind died down, the sound disappeared. *I'll go just a little bit farther,* she thought.

Dasher kept flying. She was about to turn back when she noticed a
bright, colorful glow on the horizon. Christmas lights! She flew faster.

It was everything Dasher had been dreaming of all year long.

Dasher was having so much fun, she barely noticed that it had started to snow. The sky was a blanket of white. *I'd better get home,* she thought. She looked all around for the North Star but couldn't find it anywhere. *I'm pretty sure it's this way,* she decided. And she started flying.

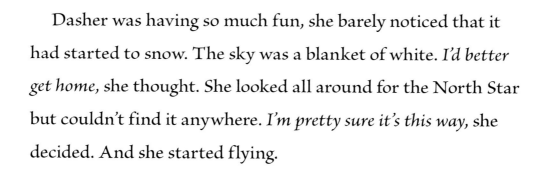

Dasher flew for a long time. She kept hoping she would remember
the way, but nothing looked familiar. She was exhausted. And hungry.

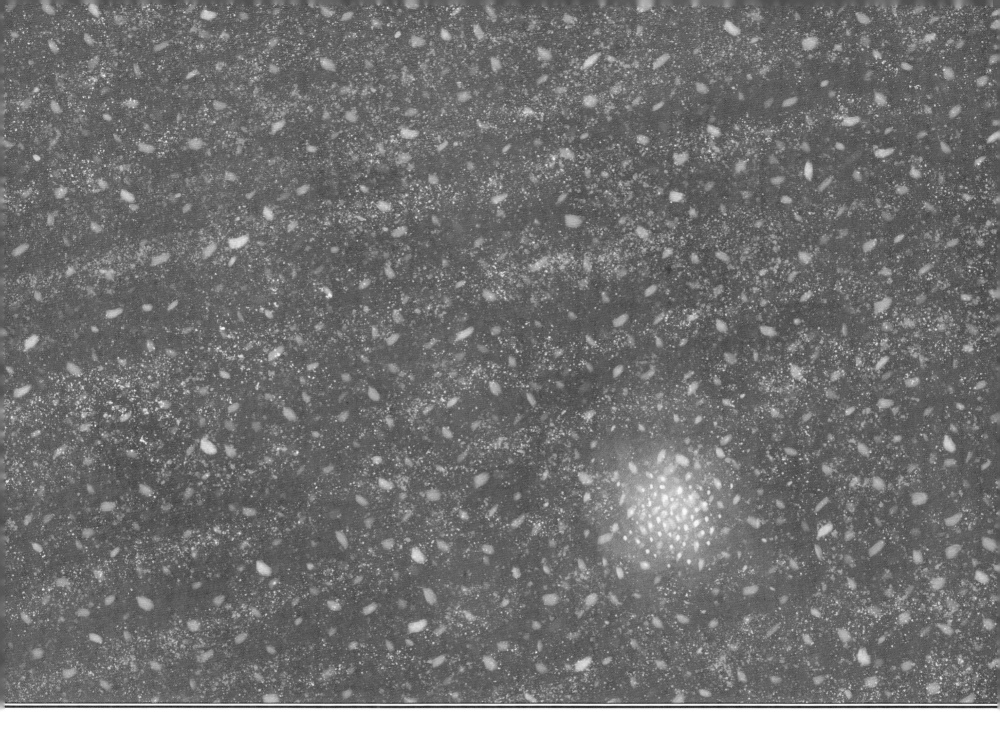

Just as she was beginning to worry, Dasher spotted something
bright in the distance.

She flew toward the light. As she got closer, she saw that it was a beautiful Christmas tree in the front yard of a little house. *I'll just rest my eyes for a minute,* she thought.

When Dasher opened her eyes, she felt blinded by the brightness. Snow still filled the sky, but now it was daytime. Suddenly, Dasher was startled by a voice.

"Good morning," said the voice.

There was a small child standing next to her, all bundled up for the storm.

"Are you one of Santa's reindeer?" asked the child.

At first, Dasher was not sure if she should answer. But then she thought about all the children she had known and how they had always been so kind to her.

Dasher nodded.

"Are you lost?" asked the child.

Dasher nodded again.

"Are you hungry?"

Dasher's stomach grumbled.

"Do you like carrots?" asked the child.

Dasher stood up.

"I'll be right back."

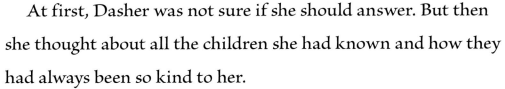

Dasher devoured a big bowlful of carrots. Then she noticed that the child was holding out a small circular object.

"You live at the North Pole, right?" asked the child.

Dasher nodded.

"Okay. This is a compass," said the child. "See that little red thing? It always points north. So if you fly that way and just keep going, you'll find your way home."

"Thank you," said Dasher.

The child's eyes widened.

"You're welcome," said the child. "And here, you can keep the compass. I think you need it more than I do. Tonight is Christmas Eve! You've got to get home!"

Dasher headed north but then turned back. "What's your name?" she asked.

The child smiled. "I'm Charlie. What's your name?"

"I'm Dasher. It was really nice to meet you, Charlie. Merry Christmas!"

"Merry Christmas, Dasher!" said Charlie. And then Dasher took to the sky.

✴

Dasher flew as fast as she could, checking the compass
every so often. Finally, the snowflakes stopped falling,
the clouds parted, and there it was—the North Star!

When Dasher arrived at the North Pole, she saw that Santa's sleigh was nearly all packed and ready.

"Dasher!" cried Mama. "Where on earth have you been?"

"I'm sorry, Mama," said Dasher. "I just . . . couldn't wait."

"Hello there, Dasher!" said Santa. "Have a bit of an adventure?"

"Yes, Santa," said Dasher. "And I know it's last minute, but I have a favor to ask."

"Ah," said Santa, "sounds serious. Let's go to the workshop. You can have some carrots and tell me all about it."

✶

That night, Dasher helped guide Santa's sleigh from rooftop to rooftop, delivering toys to children all over the world.

When Santa's sleigh landed on the rooftop of a little house with a Christmas tree in the front yard, Dasher felt more excited than ever.

"Is this the one, Dasher?" asked Santa.

"This is it," said Dasher. "Santa, could I see it one more time?"

Santa pulled out a soft velvet bag that fit perfectly in the palm of his hand. Dasher gave it a little nuzzle.

She looked at Santa and nodded, and with that, he disappeared down the chimney.

By the time they returned to the North Pole, Dasher was exhausted. She cozied up next to Mama. She wondered if Charlie was opening Christmas presents right that very minute.

"I have so much to tell you, Mama," said Dasher.

"Tomorrow, little one," said Mama.

"Okay," said Dasher. "But, Mama? How many sleeps until next Christmas?"

Mama laughed. "Merry Christmas, Dasher," she said.

"Merry Christmas, Mama," said Dasher. And she fell asleep under the glow of the North Star.